Usborne Farmyard Tales

Sticker Learning Book
Starting to read

Illustrated by Stephen Cartwright

Written by Lisa Miles
Designed by Joe Pedley

Series editor: Jenny Tyler
Consultant: Alison Kelly

Line illustrations by Guy Smith
With thanks to Heather Amery

A little yellow duck is hidden on every two pages.
When you have found the duck, you can put one of these stickers on the page.

For advice on how to use this book, see Notes for Parents on page 16.

This is Apple Tree Farm. Mrs. Boot the farmer lives here with her two children, Poppy and Sam, and a dog named Rusty.

Find the stickers to see who else lives here.

Mr. Boot **Curly** **Ted** **Woolly**

Look at the pictures below and make up a story.

Find the stickers to match these words below.

Mrs. Boot   cart   donkey   bird

The pictures of this story are in the wrong order. Can you find the right picture to go with each part of the story?

1. One day, Poppy and Sam get out their tent. They try to put it up.

2. Mrs. Boot helps them. At last, the tent is up.

3. That night, Poppy and Sam get into the tent. They are ready for bed.

4. Suddenly, the cow looks in. What a surprise!

5. The cow runs away with the tent.

6. Poppy and Sam go indoors to sleep after all.

Find the stickers to match these words.

  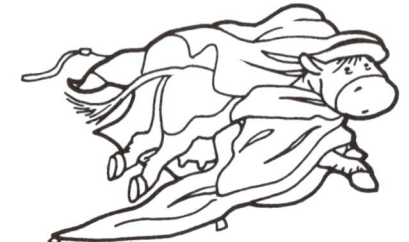 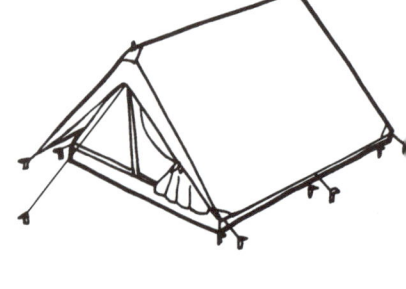

Poppy　　**Sam**　　**cow**　　**tent**

Look at each picture and say the word. Draw lines to join the words that rhyme.

 sock  ted

 goat  snake

 hat  cap

 toy  clock

 cake  coat

 bed  cat

 map  boy

Find the stickers to complete the story.

One morning, Mrs. Boot, Poppy and 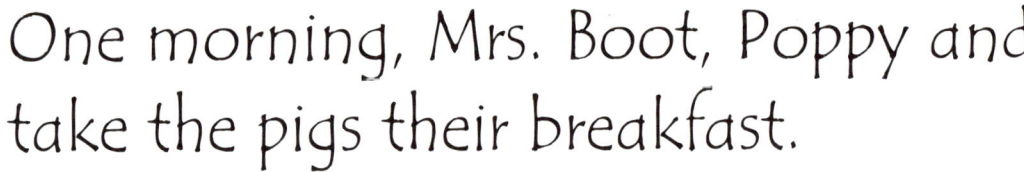 take the pigs their breakfast.

Where is Curly? He's not with the other  pigs.

Suddenly, they see him. 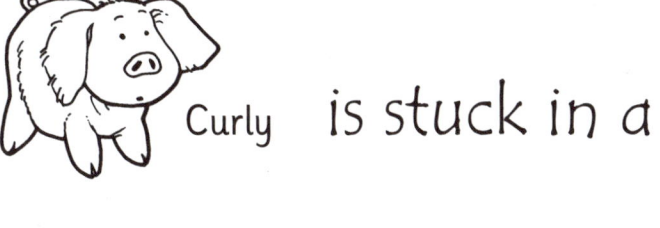 Curly is stuck in a muddy ditch.

Mrs. Boot

helps Curly. Everyone gets muddy!

Listen to the rhyming words. Find the right picture to match each sentence. Find the sticker too.

Find a bear with a pear.

Can you look for some books?

Find a boy with a toy.

Can you see a fat cat?

Find a boy with a bat and a hat.

Where's the dog with a frog?

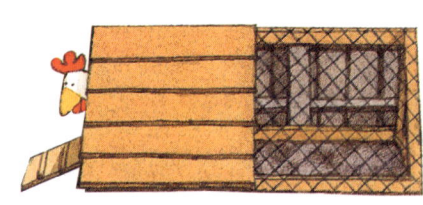

Find a hen in a pen.

What about a big pig?

8

m

Curly

Rusty

c

Sam

pigs

p

d   z

Curly

Woolly

Mrs. Boot

Can you read these words?

Say the names of the animals below. Then say the names and sounds of the letters.

Now find a letter sticker for each of these animals.

Here are some words that begin with **m**.
Find their stickers.

mouse   **man**   **milk**

Circle the word below that begins with **r**.

sheep   **dog**   **rabbit**

Circle the word below that begins with **a**.

apple   **egg**   **orange**

Circle the word below that begins with **f**.

doll   **fish**   **car**

Look at each picture and say the word. Listen to the sound the word starts with. Complete each one with either a **b** or an **s**.

......**all**   ......**un**

......**ag**    ......**oap**

Now complete each word with either a **g** or a **t**.

......**irl**   ......**able**

......**ate**   ......**owel**

Say the sound **ch**. Find the chair sticker.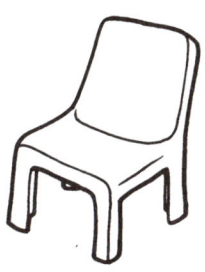

Say the sound **sh**. Find the shoe sticker.

Say the sound **th**. Find the throne sticker.

Match the words below that begin with the same sound.

chick   **shed**   **three**

thumb   **children**   **shell**

Look at each picture and say the word. Listen to the sound the word ends with. Complete each word with either a **g** or an **n**.

pi_____   twi_____

he_____   bi_____

Now complete each word with either a **k** or a **p**.

boo_____   lam_____

cu_____   for_____

What's your name? Ask someone to write your name for you here.

_____

Now copy your name in the space below.

_____

Find the name stickers for each of these Apple Tree Farm animals.

NOTES FOR PARENTS

This sticker activity book is aimed at children who are just starting to learn to read. By doing the activities with your child, you can have fun together while encouraging the development of good reading skills. Here are some points to help you and your child gain the most from this book:

You will find some simple story-telling activities, such as those on pages 2 and 3. As you read, look at the pictures and talk about them together. This will help your child to learn about stories, characters, and the way stories are shaped. It will show him or her that words and pictures fit together to tell the story.

On pages 5 and 8, there are some rhyming activities. Rhymes encourage children to listen carefully to words. Children need to be able to hear these individual sounds if they are to make successful use of phonic clues, for instance that **ph** stands for "fuh", when they come to read on their own. Singing nursery rhymes and songs, and reading poems together, are other fun things that you could do.

Other activities in this book, such as those on pages 10 and 11, help your child to recognize either simple words or individual letters. When you say the letters, give the sound that the letters make, as well as the "name" of the letter. For instance, tell your child that the letter **b** says "buh". By learning the sounds, children will find it easier to tackle words that they don't know when they begin to read on their own.

On page 15, there is a space for your child to write his or her own name. Children develop a strong interest in their names and often learn to recognize these letters first. Above all, read to your child as much as you possibly can. This is the most important way that you can introduce children to the enjoyment and rewards of reading. It also begins to teach them about the structure and language of stories.

Always make sure that your child is still enjoying the activities. You can always stop and come back to them later.

Wherever you see a black and white picture in this book, there is a sticker to match.

The alphabet

On the inside covers of this book are the letters of the alphabet for your child to draw over. Make sure that they start each letter at the correct place, and follow the directions of the arrows as shown below when writing the letters.

a b c d e f g h i j k l m
n o p q r s t u v w x y z

Table of Contents - Volume I

Jazz Tunes For Improvisation

Track	Selection	Composer	Track Length	Page
1.	Doobee	Petersen	4:05	4
2.	Evening Sunset	Petersen	4:59	5
3.	Crib Chimp	Haerle	4:12	6
4.	Spiral	Petersen	3:38	7
5.	Big Foot Bossa	Haerle	3:40	8
6.	Mr. Lionel	Matteson	4:28	9
7.	Cupcake	Petersen	4:08	10
8.	Holly	Matteson	3:57	11
9.	Mutton Stew	Matteson	3:53	12
10.	My Little P.B.	Matteson	4:31	13
11.	Bebop Baby	Haerle	3:56	14
12.	Tripod Revisited	Matteson	3:43	15
13.	Skippin'	Petersen	4:07	16
14.	Night Mood	Petersen	3:33	17
15.	Roman Glee	Haerle	4:51	18
16.	Kee Bop	Haerle	5:49	19
17.	Once Upon A Time	Haerle	4:10	20
			71:40 (Total Time)	
	Appendix			21

© 1983, 1988 STUDIO 224 (ASCAP) This Edition © 1997 STUDIO 224
All Rights Administered by WARNER BROS. PUBLICATIONS U.S. INC.
All Rights Reserved including Public Performance for Profit

Any duplication, adaptation or arrangement of the compositions
contained in this collection requires the written consent of the Publisher.
No part of this book may be photocopied or reproduced in any way without permission.
Unauthorized uses are an infringement of U.S. Copyright Act and are punishable by Law.

Introduction - Volume I

The purpose of this book is to provide resource materials for the study of improvisation, either individually or in a class situation. The tunes included here are based on typical kinds of chord progressions found in many jazz standards or on special types of progressions that have been found by the authors to be valuable for study. The melodies are designed as typical examples of melodic motion through various kinds of harmonies. These tunes have been used in class situations with good success for several years before arriving at the final decision to use them here. Many tunes which proved ineffective for study were discarded and are not included.

Generally speaking, the tunes are arranged in order of difficulty. This is especially true in book one. In the early stages, it has been found that the most solid kind of growth takes place by proceeding through certain kinds of problems in a rather specific order. In some cases, it is hard to say which tunes are more or less difficult since each may present quite different kinds of problems. However, an individual or class will probably find that moving through the book in page order produces the best results.

It is the authors' hope that, by providing students with tunes which have accurate chord changes and melodies as well as accompaniment tracks to practice with, an important need will be met in the area of improvisational materials. Moreover, it is the authors' desire that students in educational situations feel free to use any of these tunes as vehicles for writing and performance (with the publisher's permission) as long as there is no financial gain realized through said use.

The first part of this book includes tunes which are based on harmonies of long duration and which initially involve only one or two scale forms. These scales are the most commonly used jazz modes and occur in the following order:

1) Dorian mode (pure minor scale with a raised 6th scale step)
2) Mixolydian mode (major scale with a lowered 7th scale step)
3) Dorian and mixolydian modes together
4) Ionian mode (major scale)
5) Dorian, mixolydian and ionian modes together

The following example shows that C Dorian, C Mixolydian and C Ionian scales:

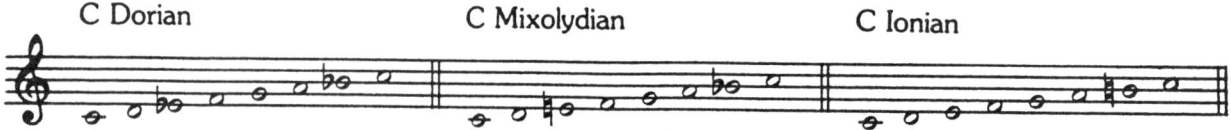

Volume I (cont.)

The fifth category of tunes also introduces the II-V-I progression in a major key, one of the most common of all jazz chord progressions.

Students should stress diatonic playing (free of chromatic embellishment) until each mode is firmly fixed in both their minds and fingers. Once the tones of a particular scale are set, then chromaticism may be used sparingly. It is also important to stress the 3rds and 7ths of chords to identify the harmony for the listener. In addition, certain chord (scale) tones also require care in handling:

> 1) The 4th scale step in an ionian or mixolydian scale should move stepwise to the 3rd or 5th if the 4th isn't suspended in the chord.
> 2) The 4th scale step may be stressed if it is suspended in the chord.
> 3) It is better to stress the 7th or 9th (2nd) scale step in an ionian scale rather than the root.

Refer to the appendix of this book for more information on chord/scale relationships.

The later section of this book includes tunes which are based on harmonies of shorter duration. There are many examples present of the II-V-I progression in a major key. Often only the II-V or V-I portion of the progression is used. It is important to learn to identify the relationship of a minor 7th chord (IImi7) moving down a perfect 5th to a dominant 7th chord (V7) and then down a perfect 5th to the major key center (Ima7). This key center can be felt (heard) even if the I chord does not occur.

Also, in this section, the II-V-I progression in a minor key is introduced. This consists of a minor 7th chord with a lowered 5th (IImi7-5) moving down a perfect 5th to a dominant 7th chord with a lowered 9th and 13th (V7-9-13) and then down a perfect 5th to the minor key center (Imi7). As before, this key center can be felt (heard) even if the I chord does not occur.

This section also includes tunes which introduce other modes of the major scale (phrygian, lydian, aeolian and locrian), the whole tone and diminished scales, and modes of the harmonic and melodic minor scales. Consult the scale syllabus found in the appendix of this book for explanation of the various chord/scale relationships.

Doobee

Jack Petersen

Evening Sunset

JACK PETERSEN

Eb

Crib Chimp

Eb

DAN HAERLE

LATIN-FUNK ♩=144

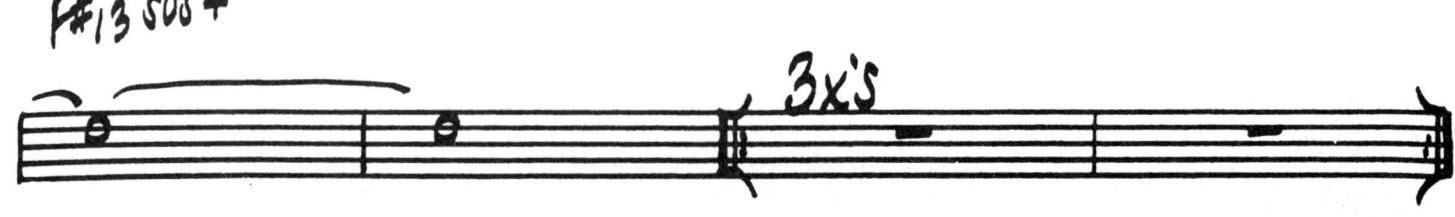

Spiral

JACK PETERSEN

Med. Swing ♩=176

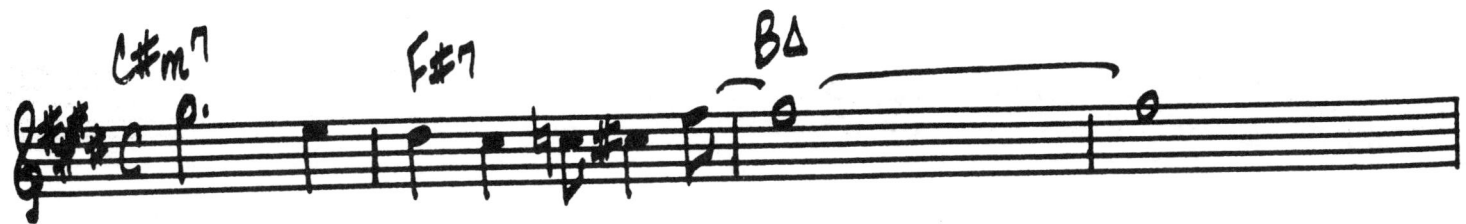

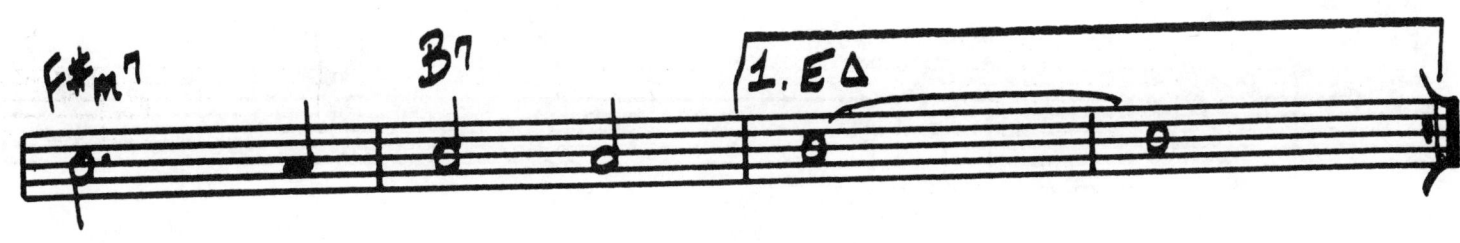

8

Eb

Big Foot Bossa

DAN HAERLE

Bossa Nova ♩= 132

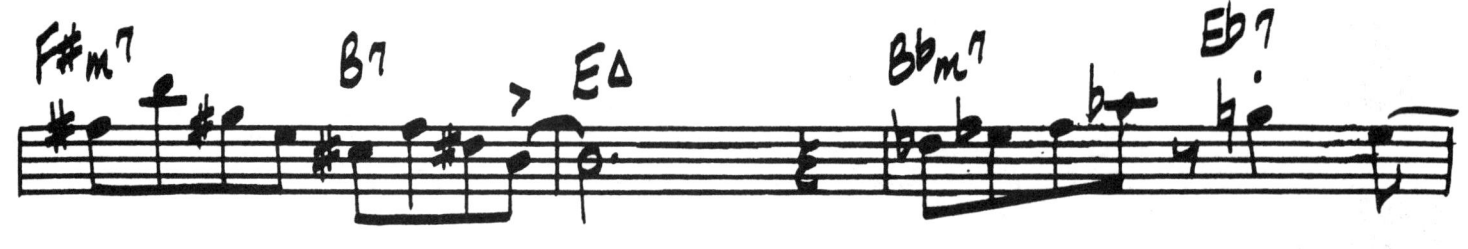

Mr. Lionel

RICH MATTESON

Cupcake

JACK PETERSEN

Eb

Fast Swing ♩= 120

My Little P. B.

Bebop Baby

Eb

DAN HAERLE

Skippin'

JACK PETERSEN

Eb

Night Mood

JACK PETERSEN

Eb

Eb

Roman Glee

DAN HAERLE

Bossa Nova ♩= 152

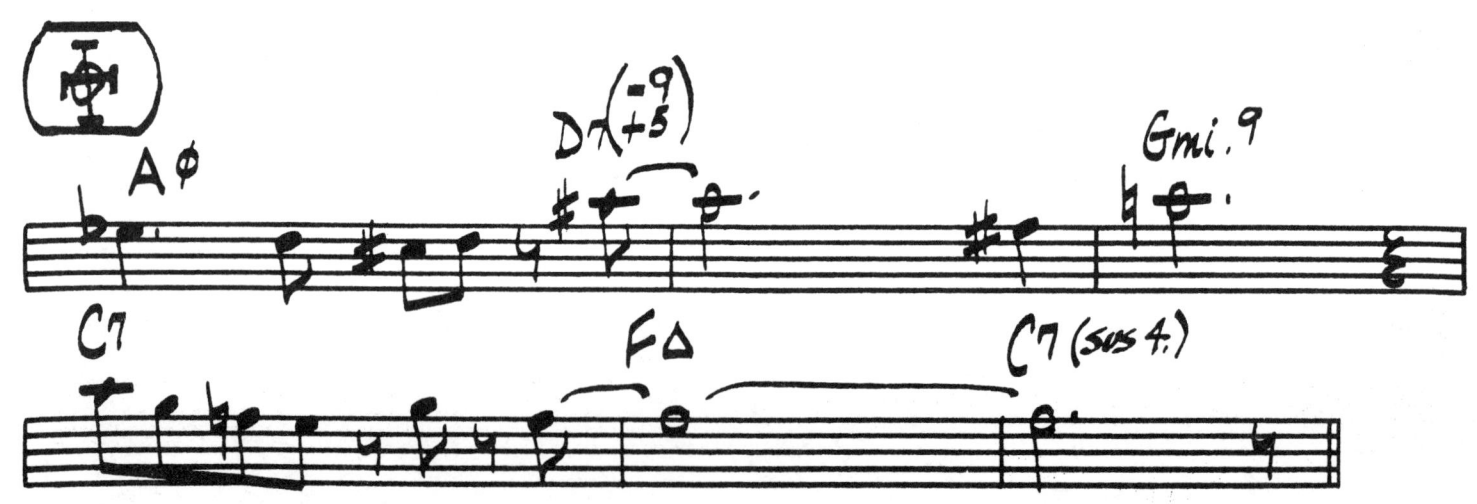

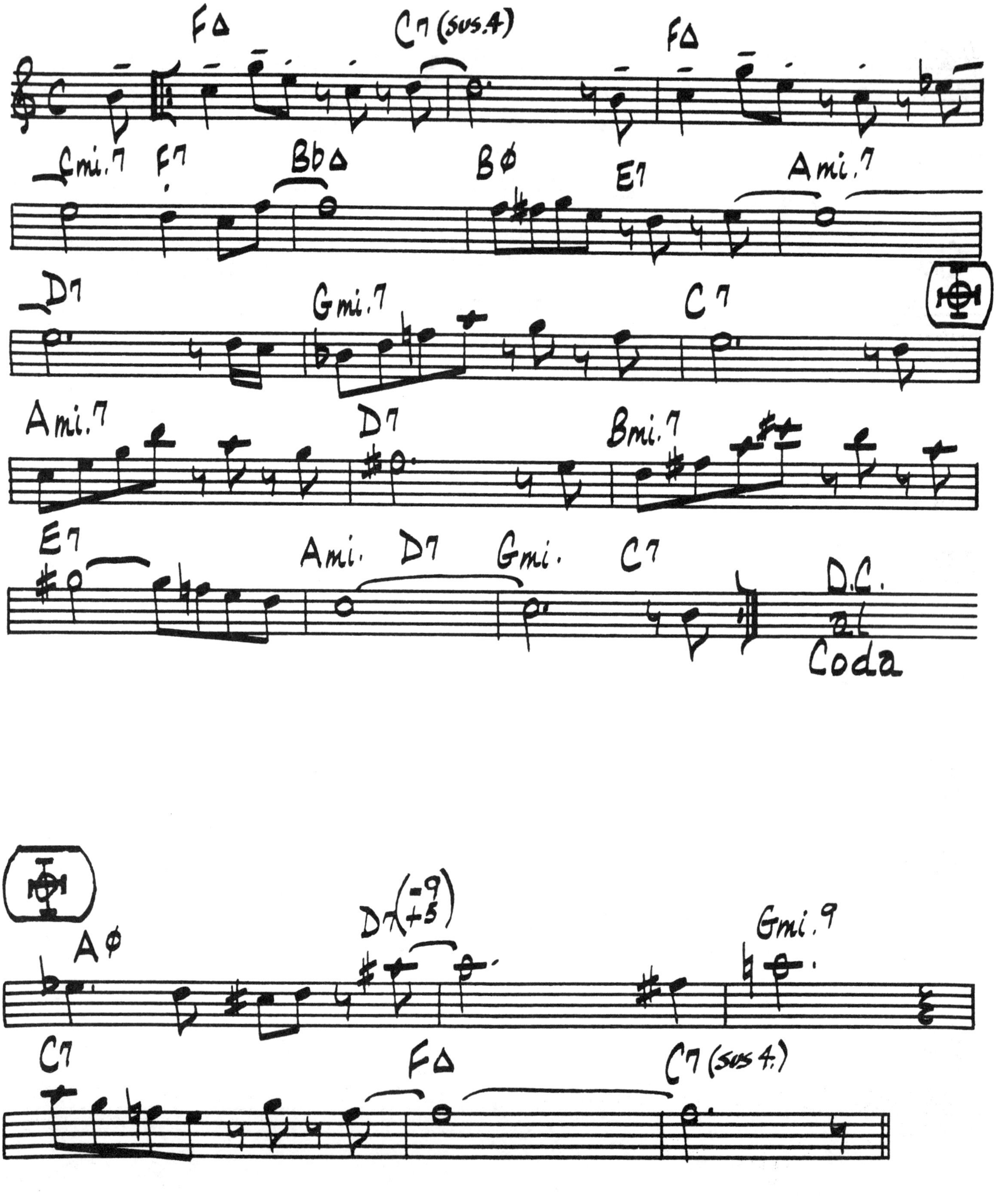

Kee Bop

Eb

DAN HAERLE

Once Upon A Time

Eb

DAN HAERLE

- APPENDIX -

Nomenclature (in the key of C for comparison)

Major family: C, C6, C69, C△, C△9, C△9+11, C△13, C△+5

Minor family: Cmi, Cmi7, Cmi9, Cmi11, Cmi13, Cmi#7

Dominant family: C7, C9, C13, C7sus4, C7-5, C7+5, C7+11, C7-13, C7-9, C7+9, or an combination of alterations.

Half-diminished 7th: Cmi7-5 or C∅

Fully diminished 7th: °7 or dim7

Diminished major 7th: dim△7

Scale Syllabus (arranged in order of need)

Chord family	Function	Scale choice	Example
minor	I or VI	Aeolian	
minor	II or IV	Dorian	
minor	III	Phrygian	
minor	Any	Minor pentatonic	
minor	I	Blues	
minor, #7	I	Ascending Melodic minor	
minor, #7	I	Harmonic minor	

Chord family	Alterations	Scale choice	Example
dominant	unaltered	Mixolydian	
dominant	suspended 4th	Mixolydian	
dominant	-5 or +5	Whole Tone	
dominant	+11	Lydian, 7	
dominant	-13	5th mode melodic minor	
dominant	-9 or +9	Half-whole diminished	
dominant	+9	Blues	
dominant	-9 and -13	5th mode harmonic minor	
dominant	any combination of altered 5th and 9th	Super Locrian	

Chord family	Function	Scale Choice
major	I	Ionian
major	IV	Lydian
major	VI	6th mode harmonic
major	any	Major pentatonic
major, #5	any	Lydian Augmented
major, #5	any	Augmented
major, #5	any	3rd mode harmonic

Chord family	Function	Scale choice	Example
minor 7th, -5	II or VII	Locrian	
minor 7th, -5	II	2nd mode harmonic	
minor 9th, -5	II	Locrian, #2	
diminished 7th	VII	7th mode harmonic	
diminished 7th	VII	Whole-half diminished	
diminished, #7	any	Whole-half diminished	